N

GREER ELEMENTARY SCHOOL Book Room
2055 LAMBS ROAD
CHARLOTTESVILLE, VA

bookroom

P9-EGM-776

POINSETTLA & HER FAMILY

Felicia Bond

A Harper Trophy Book

Harper & Row, Publishers

Copyright © 1981 by Felicia Bond
All rights reserved. Printed in the United States of America.
No part of this book may be used or reproduced in any manner
whatsoever without written permission except in the case of
brief quotations embodied in critical articles and reviews.
For information address Thomas Y. Crowell Junior Books, 10 East 53rd Street,
New York, N.Y. 10022. Published simultaneously in Canada by
Fitzhenry & Whiteside Limited, Toronto.

Library of Congress Cataloging in Publication Data
Bond, Felicia.
    Poinsettia and her family.

    Summary: Poinsettia Pig thinks the house she
lives in would be perfect without her noisy,
messy, always-in-the-way brothers and sisters.
    [1. Brothers and sisters—Fiction.   2. Pigs
—Fiction.   I. Title.
PZ7.B6366Po 1981   [E]   81–43035
ISBN 0–690–04144–6   AACR2
ISBN 0–690–04145–4   (lib. bdg.)
ISBN 0–06–443076–6   (pbk.)

Published in hardcover by
Thomas Y. Crowell, New York.

To my father, Oliver James Bond

Poinsettia had six brothers and sisters, a mother, and a father.

They lived in a fine, old house surrounded by hydrangea bushes and lilac hedges, which Poinsettia's mother would occasionally cut for a nice effect in the dining room.

There was pachysandra in which to play hide-and-seek in the early evenings of summer, and a rock out front to sit on.

Inside, there was a red leather window seat for reading in the late afternoon sun, and a bathroom with balloon-pink wallpaper. Poinsettia thought it a perfect house.

One day, Poinsettia came home from the library with her favorite book, a book about a little, spotted circus horse who danced. Poinsettia had read it five times before, but she was looking forward to it all the same.

She trotted past her mother in the garden and her father in the kitchen, and headed straight for the red leather window seat.

If the sun was coming in the window just right, it would spread like warm butter across the pages of her book. Poinsettia walked a little faster, patting her pocket to make sure it held the cherry tart she had bought for just this occasion.

The sun was coming in the window just right, but it
was spreading like warm butter across the fat, little
body of Julius, the third from the youngest, who was
already curled up on the soft red leather.

"I will go to the rock in the front yard," Poinsettia grunted, "where I can read my book in peace."

But the rock could hardly be seen for all the piglets lying about. "Like a bunch of seals," Poinsettia snorted.

She stomped off toward the balloon-pink bathroom, where the tub was just right for reading. But there, up to her chins in water, was Chick Pea, who said she hadn't washed her feet yet.

"This house would be perfect except for one thing," Poinsettia fumed. "There are too many of us in it! It is not possible to go anywhere without running into a brother or a sister, a mother or a father!"

That night, Poinsettia was very nasty. She pinched a brother, stepped on a sister, and yelled louder than both of them put together.

She did more things and worse things, and it was only seven o'clock.

Poinsettia was sent to bed early that night for general misbehavior.

The next day, Poinsettia's father announced to the whole family that they were moving. "We will look for a new house," he said. "This one is too small for us."

"Oh, no, it's not," Poinsettia thought. "It's the family that's too big." But she kept her thoughts to herself and vowed not to go with them.

When the family left, Poinsettia lay low in the pachysandra. Nobody noticed. The car seemed full.

She lay there a long time, just in case they came back. They didn't.

"Good!" Poinsettia said and, clutching her book close to her, ran straight for the red leather window seat.

The light had never been more buttery, nor the leather as warm. Poinsettia read two pages there, then ran to the rock in the front yard. The rock had never felt more solid.

Poinsettia read six more pages. But a wind was whipping up, and it was even starting to snow. Poinsettia ran inside.

She warmed herself in a deliciously hot bath. She read four pages, then spent an hour staring dreamily at the wallpaper. It had never looked pinker, and neither had Poinsettia.

"I'm a pig in bliss," she gurgled.

Poinsettia let the water out of the tub.

The snow came down harder, and Poinsettia fell asleep. She dreamed about the dancing circus horse.

It snowed all that afternoon and into the evening. By the time it was dark, Poinsettia had read her book eighteen times. She wrapped herself in an old blanket and looked for something to eat. What little food there was she ate cold.

"The house is not as it used to be," she said aloud quietly.

"What I need is a rope! If I had a rope, I could make a tent with this blanket. I could tie the rope to two doorknobs and put the blanket over it. My tent would be a house inside a house. What a good idea."

Poinsettia searched everywhere for a bit of rope. All she found was a frayed piece of string that was barely long enough for anything.

But in the farthest corner of a dark, dark closet, Poinsettia found something else. It was a photograph, an old photograph of her family. Poinsettia remembered taking it herself.

This was too much for Poinsettia.

With the point of her hoof, she very carefully made a little hole in the top of the photograph. Through the hole she threaded the string she had found. On each end she made a knot.

"This is all I have left of my family!" Poinsettia
cried, and cried, and cried.

"Poinsettia!" a small voice called. "Poinsettia!"
Poinsettia nearly fainted dead away.

There were her six brothers and sisters, her mother and her father, all squashed and crowded together and smiling from ear to ear!

"We would have been back sooner," Poinsettia's father said, "but the car got stuck in the snow. It's a good thing there are so many of us. We all got out and pushed."

"Pierre counted everyone, but he counted wrong because he's only three," said Petunia, the oldest.

"I don't know why we didn't notice right away that you were missing," Julius said, "because everything was so peaceful."

"The whole time we were gone, Poinsettia," her mother said, "we talked about what a wonderful house this is. It is our home. Perhaps we don't need as much room as we thought."

"Maybe not," Poinsettia said.

And shoulder to shoulder, elbow to elbow, all squashed and crowded together, they spent the rest of that night,

and many other nights together... as together as nine
pigs could be...

in their fine, old house.